The Rise and Fall of Claude the Magnificent

WRITTEN BY

Chris Capstick

ILLUSTRATED BY

Monika Filipina

Claude was a country cat, but unlike his brothers and sisters who were fierce hunters and fearless acrobats, Claude was an *artiste*.

He loved to paint, sculpt and
create beautiful things.

When he was old enough his mother said to him,
"The country is no place for a cat like you. You must take
your talents to Paris and become rich and famous!"

So the very next day, Claude packed his few
belongings and set off for the big city.

From far away, Paris had looked beautiful and peaceful, but up close it was quite different.

The bustling streets were crammed with busy shops and noisy stalls.

Claude began to ask around,
"Where can an *artiste* find work in these parts?"
But everyone either ignored him or laughed in his face.

For weeks he tried without success, and having no money for food or a room, he slept the nights away in doorways and rummaged through rubbish for scraps to eat.

One night, he disturbed an old cat
who was asleep at the bottom of a bin.

"I too came to Paris to seek my fame
and fortune. But these people don't want
art from poor country cats – they want it
from famous *artistes* like Pablo Picatto,
Rafael and Leonardo Dog Vinci."

"To be a success, you must think of
something the people need,
then make it irresistible!"

Claude racked his brains all night long – he had lots of ideas
but never quite the right one.

At midnight, he decided to go for a walk to clear his head.

Not looking where he was going, he stepped out into the middle of the road – right into the path of a horse!

The shocked horse reared up, Claude stumbled and fell!

As he lay on the cobbles about to be squashed, his idea finally came.

And what an idea it was!

For as he looked up at the horse's foot, Claude thought, "If horses can wear shoes, why can't CATS wear HATS!"

Claude made a lucky escape (he is a cat you know!) and got straight to work making three beautiful hats from thrown away scraps.

Within an hour he had sold them to three
dancing can-can cats.

With some money at last, Claude had
a tasty meal of milk and cheese...

...He took a cosy room in
a small house...

...And bought some fine materials
to make more hats.

Word got around and very soon
the cats of Paris were lining up
for one of Claude's hats.

Les Chapeaux de Claude

Claude soon had enough money to open a shop where he employed assistant *artistes* to help him with his creations.

Customers came from far and wide –
Sultans and Princesses, Sopranos and
Bishops, Viennese Musicians and Eastern
Mystics all sought out Claude.

His designs became so extravagant and flamboyant
that the city's streets and monuments had to be
made wider to accommodate his art.

But as Claude's creations grew ever bigger, so did his ego.
He began to forget his humble beginnings and scoffed at
poorer cats who only wanted smaller hats.

The rich and famous
continued to seek him out.

He created a pyramid hat
for the Pharaoh...

...A galleon on the crest of a
wave for the Admiral,

...And a giant ice sculpture of wrestling polar bears for the Queen of the Eskimos.

Then the street cat
talked to the waiter...

...who mentioned
to the house maid...

...who whispered
to the chef...

...who spoke to
the butler...

...who finally told the King of France all about Claude's fabulous work.

The King announced that Claude would receive caskets of gold,
a castle and titles if he could create for the King the most enormously
extravagant hat the world had ever seen.

Greedily, Claude agreed and began work without delay.

"This hat will be my masterpiece! It will be so massively lavish and exquisite that it must be built in a place for all of Paris to see."

On seeing their master's plan, Claude's assistants warned him that such a huge hat could hurt someone.

"What do you know?" he sneered.

"I am Claude – THE MAGNIFICENT!"

For weeks he worked and plied his craft, building the monstrous hat. Finally it was hoisted aloft by a huge crane to hang over a golden throne, ready for the King to sit on.

At the ceremony, the King waved regally to the gathered crowds as Claude announced the grand unveiling.

But just as Claude was about to lower the
hat onto the King's head – DISASTER!

The chain snapped, the colossal hat fell
and the King was squashed flat!

Claude was ruined.

After the incident with the King, nobody would buy his hats – not even small ones.

With no money, he once more had to sleep in doorways and nibble thrown-away scraps.

He finally returned home to the countryside
where he spent the rest of his days making
sensible clogs for country dogs.

And the King...?

...He still lies quite squashed beneath the hat, though all that remains of Claude's enormous creation is its rather distinctive steel frame.

Be sure to go and see it, if you ever visit Paris.